TONY ENGLE

Sweety Tweety
BOOKS

Sweety Tweety Books titles may be ordered from your favorite bookseller.
www.SweetyTweety.com

Sweety Tweety Books
c/o CMI Fulfillment
4822 South 133rd Street, Suite 200, Omaha, NE 68137

Paperback: 978-1-945505-11-9

LCCN and Library of Congress cataloging in publication data on file with publisher.

Printed in the USA

10 9 8 7 6 5 4 3 2 1

Introduction

This was developed because of my experiences with baseball. Anthony met a professional speed skater who could only see the line of the skating rink below him. He spoke at the vending convention for the blind and told how dreams are possible. Anthony played beeper ball for the blind and visited Wrigley Field for a few games, plus Mynan Field for a few minor League games with the Peoria Chiefs.

This book is solely for enjoyment and excitement, with the names and places coincidental. Russel Smith is the only pitcher who's visually impaired to make the Big Show with a good deal of accomplishment and self-doubt, as he tells of his experiences throughout baseball. The tension and drama build as Russel talks about his persistence with support from his family, friends, and those in the sports world.

Chapter 1

Hello everyone, I'm Russel Smith from Peoria, Illinois, and I was born to Charles and Tammy Smith. I'm six foot one, and 195 pounds. My mother is five foot six and weighs 150 pounds. My father is six foot two and weighs 210 pounds, and we have light brown hair and blue eyes. I have no sight except for light perception and wear a Cubs jersey with the logo and number eleven on the back. I have two brothers and a sister who live in Springfield, Illinois. Charles Jr. is a little shorter, five foot ten with light brown hair and blue eyes and weighs 180 pounds. Tom is five foot seven and weighs 165 pounds. Donna is five foot seven with long dark blond hair and blue eyes and weighs 140 pounds. My hobbies and interests include sports such as bowling, swimming, hockey, auto racing, basketball, football, baseball, and blues music.

My first experience with baseball was visiting Wrigley Field and following the careers of Ron Santo, Billy Williams, Ernie Banks and so on.

"How big is the crowd, Dad?" I ask as a 10-year-old boy.

"Son, the crowd looks like about 39,000 to 45,000 people here, and maybe you could be pitching for the Cubs," answers Father.

I sit with Dad on the bleachers as Dave Kingman comes to the plate with Jerry Mumphrey aboard. Harry Carry is on the radio next to us with the announcement: "Kingman waits at the plate for the first pitch from Rex Sutcliff, curve ball, strike on the outside corner. The outfield is deep around this beautiful sunny day with the infield back. Here comes the zero and one count pitch, inside with the fastball, and Kingman steps out, choking up on the bat. Here comes the 1 and 1 count, fastball, and there's a long drive, way back, back, it is a home run over the center field wall for 2 runs, and the Cubs beat the Cardinals 3 to 2! Holy cow!"

The weather in Chicago is sunny with very few clouds in the sky and the temperature around 80 to 85 degrees. "That is sweet," I tell my father.

Mother is home cooking when we get back from Chicago. "How is Wrigley Field?" she asks.

"Russel had the time of his life," says my father to my mother.

"I want to be a pitcher, mother," I say.

The house smells of fried chicken, fried potatoes, and cake which is set on the table for dessert. "How is it possible?" asks mom.

"We'll talk about this during the school year," answers father.

The end of August comes, and it's time to go back to school with the hot and muggy weather for a month. "I want to play baseball," I say to my friend Scott.

He pauses a little and says, "You're blind. How can you play?"

I feel disappointed and tell my dad. "Look, son, we'll get through this because technology has come a long way. You know I work with computers, and they talk for the blind," reassures father. The solution is I'll wear earbuds with a device that's used for hearing aids and a wireless microphone for the catcher to announce where the ball will be located to keep the batters off balance.

My grades are pretty good during the winter, and finally, spring comes with the flowers blooming and trees developing leaves.

Coach Mac, a man of six foot two and 225 pounds, says, "We can't sign you because you're blind and will be against school policy." I handed the coach's note to my parents saying that I'm not allowed to pitch on the team because I'm blind, and they decided that a visit to the school was necessary.

The plan is scheduled for March 1st with principal Gipson, who is six foot, brown eyes, blond hair, and 210 pounds. "Hi, we're Charles and Tammy Smith. We are here on behalf of my son who was told that he can't pitch baseball because of his blindness. Can you explain why?" asks my father.

"Glad to meet you folks. The reason he's not allowed to play baseball is because school policy prohibits visually impaired people from playing sports," replies Mr. Gipson.

"That does not comply with the American Disabilities Act," says father.

Mr. Gipson gives my parents a dirty look. "Get out of my office!" he says with emotion.

Their faces are angry as they leave his office to consult with their lawyer, Tim Swanson. Mr. Swanson is five foot ten with red hair and blue eyes and wears a light brown sports jacket, brown pants, and brown shoes. The office is twenty feet by twenty feet inside the First National Bank Building in the town's business area.

"Hi, glad you can come; how can we help you?" asks Mr. Swanson. "We're Charles and Tammy Smith, and we're here on behalf of my son Russel, who has been informed that he can't pitch baseball because the school doesn't allow visually impaired people to play sports," says my mother.

"Have you talked with the school board?" asks Mr. Swanson.

"No, we have not," says Father.

"I need something from them, and we'll go from that point," says Mr. Swanson. I don't understand everything they are saying because I'm still young.

My parents show relief and say, "Thank you, Mr. Swanson, we'll get something done about this situation."

They make an appointment with the school board to discuss the policy. When they enter the building, a public meeting is just starting its session. This location is on the school's second floor, which is lined with classrooms, but the auditorium is full of parents and faculty.

"The meeting will come to order," remarks Mr. Nick Clayborne, a man of five foot eleven with brown hair and hazel eyes.

"Is there any new business?"

My father gets up to speak, "Ladies and gentlemen, we believe that many visually impaired children want to play sports, including my son, because they feel normal." There is silence in the room after he finishes speaking, and the parents are surprised.

"Our son Russel wants to play baseball and live a productive life," my mother said.

"The meeting is adjourned," says Mr. Clayborne and the crowd shuffles out of the building. Mr. Nick Clayborne stops to talk with my father and mother. "I understand that visually impaired people like sports, but safety is our concern," he says.

"Look, aren't you overreacting? Visually impaired children are no more dangerous than children with full sight," says my mother.

"There is no more discussion, and this matter is closed," says Mr. Clayborne.

My parents leave the building and decide to seek signatures from parents of visually impaired children and give them to Mr. Swanson.

"Mr. and Mrs. Smith, it looks like discrimination charges will be filed unless the district is willing to settle this out of court," says Mr. Swanson.

"We want better lives for these children because my son wants to play baseball and be in the Major Leagues one day," says father. Mr. Swanson looks over his notes and sends copies of the signatures by email to all the schools in the District.

My parents wait for the school board to adopt a new policy and learn that I and the other children are allowed to play sports.

Chapter 2

I go to the mound for the first time with my device and earbuds while the team cheers.

"This is Marlin Fox in Peoria, Illinois. We're here to witness Russel Smith pitch baseball. There will be more information after the game."

Russel's father and mother look on as Russel begins his wind-up.

"This is Kurt Davis announcing the game and there's a fastball as a strike, and the game is underway.

Larry Hill is catching for Russel Smith. "Need a curve ball," he whispers into the wireless microphone. The wind-up and the pitch. It's low and outside, with the curve.

The crowd watches in amazement as Smith deals the 1 and 1 count: swing, and there's a drive, way back… it's long enough and gone! It's a home run! Pekin, Illinois, scores the 1st run of the game and Coach Mac comes to the mound.

"It's okay, Russ," he says, putting his hand on Smith's shoulder. "I realize you're a good pitcher and keep up the good work. How are you feeling?"

I paused a little: "Coach, I feel embarrassed but ready." The crowd cheers as Coach Mac walks back to the dugout and play resumes.

"Curveball low and outside," remarks Larry."

The batter waits for the first pitch: outside and low with the curve." announces Mr. Davis. "Russel Smith deals the 0 and 1 count: strike on the inside corner with the fastball at 35 miles per hour. The crowd cheers and claps as Smith delivers the 0 and 2 pitch: swing and a miss as the batter throws his bat down in disgust. The batter charges the mound as cameras flash, and the umpire comes over to prevent a potential fight.

"Break it up, young man," the umpire says with authority to the batter, Brian Sampson.

"It's unfair!" yells Sampson.

"You stupid jerk!" he yells again, pointing to Russel.

Larry Hill comes out to talk to Russel. "It's okay, man; the umpire comes out before he starts something. You all right?" he asks, worried.

"Yeah, I'm afraid that batter might hit me!" replies Russel as he trembles.

"You are ejected from the game," says Mr. Norris, the umpire, to Sampson.

Sampson is angry as the coach of Pekin leads him out toward the locker room.

Smith begins his warm-up tosses with Larry Hill. "It's okay, need a fastball," Larry says into the microphone.

It's now the bottom of the ninth inning with Thomas Jefferson School up to bat and the crowd cheering with runners on first and second because of a single and a walk, and here comes Lee Williams to the plate.

Kurt Davis announces: "Pekin's pitcher, Jack Hernandes pitches to Williams, change-up strike on the outside corner. Here comes the 0 and 1 count: low and inside with the fast-ball, and Williams steps out, taking practice cuts with his bat. The outfield is deep for Lee Williams who is stocky at nine years old. The infield is back looking for the double play as Hernandez deals the 1 and 1 count: swing and there's a drive, way back, way back, it might be, it could be a towering home run as the crowd gets to its feet! Holy cow while the players and coaches from both teams gather on the field to shake hands and Thomas Jefferson wins the game 3 to 1!"

My parents and I are excited as we move among the crowd.

"That is great!" I say to my mother.

"We worried that boy would charge toward you at the mound," says Mother.

"I'm worried, Mom, but thank God for the umpire and coaches," I say with relief.

"Excuse me, I'm looking for Russel Smith," says Marlin Fox. "I'm Marlin Fox of Peoria radio, and I would like an interview."

"How do you do?" asks father.

"We're Charles and Tammy Smith and this is our son Russel," says mother.

"Congratulations, Russel, but why are you wearing earbuds during the game?" asks Mr. Fox.

"I'm blind and want to play baseball like other people," I say.

"We adapted the technology so the catcher and Russel know where the ball should go and how it should be thrown to keep the batters off balance. He wants to be in the Majors," explains father.

"We're witnessing a moment in history, and we thank you folks," says Mr. Fox. "This is Marlin Fox of Peoria radio reporting."

Chapter 3

I was to participate in Little League, but I discovered they had problems with my lack of sight. Coach Patterson, who stands five foot eleven in a replica of the Cubs uniform, 190 pounds with brown hair, brown eyes and a mustache says, "Son we can't sign you because we won't allow blind kids to play, and good luck with other activities."

My friend Scott's parents take me home with the bad news.

"Scott is upset with what happened to Russel." says Mr. Hanson, who is five foot nine, 175 pounds, with blond hair, brown eyes and a clean-shaven face. He wears blue jeans and a shirt from the Caterpillar plant.

"We're told that Russel can't play because he's blind, and Coach Patterson wished him good luck with other activities," says Mrs. Hanson.

"We know that Russel can play because we watched him," says Mr. Hanson.

Scott and I are dropped off at Larry's house while my parents and the Hansons visit our lawyer, Mr. Swanson. Mrs. Hanson is five foot one, 115 pounds and wears a pink blouse, slacks, with makeup over her brown eyes and has long dark blond hair. The weather outside is seventy-five degrees and sunny, with wind gusting to fifteen miles.

"Hi, glad to see you again; how can we help you today?" asks Mr. Swanson.

"These are our friends, Mr. and Mrs. Hanson, and we're here to report that our son Russel is told that he can't pitch in Little League," says father.

"I saw Russel pitch, and I'll email Coach Anderson to make an appointment to discuss the issue," says Mr. Swanson. "I'm sorry, I mean Coach Patterson."

Mr. Patterson agrees and arrives quickly after the email is received. "What's this about?" he asks.

"I'm Mr. Swanson, the attorney representing the Smiths, and it's come to my attention that you won't let their son play baseball because he's blind. Is that correct?" asks Mr. Swanson.

"Yes, because safety is our concern, and he can't see where to throw the ball to the batters," says Mr. Patterson.

"Have you dealt with blind people before?" asks my father.

"It's okay, Charles," reassures Mother.

"Mr. Patterson, we recommend that you comply with the American Disabilities Act, or the alternative is to shut down your League for discrimination," says Mr. Swanson.

Mr. Patterson rises from his chair without shaking hands with anyone and is angry, heading to the door. "You will hear from my lawyer!" says Mr. Patterson as he slams the door behind him. Mr. Swanson looks over his notes to ensure he writes down all parts of the conversation.

"There will be discrimination charges filed, and in the meantime, your son will have to keep practicing his pitches," says Mr. Swanson. The Smiths and Hansons shake hands with Mr. Swanson and thank him for his time. "We'll keep you posted on any developments.".

My father, mother, and the Hansons get up from their chairs and head back to Larry's house to pick me and Scott up to go home. We drop off Scott, and when my parents pull in the driveway. Suddenly, a shot rings out from across the street, and a bullet strikes my leg.

"Ouch! My leg! My leg!" I shout and fall like I'm on hinges.

"Russel! Russel!" My mother screams as my father looks over to see where the shot came from.

"It's all right Russel; stay there!" says father firmly. "I caught a glimpse of who it was."

"We're calling the police and medical staff right away. Stay calm," says mother. I stay still while the police and paramedics surround me.

"Did you get a description?" asks an officer to my dad.

"The gun looked like a twenty-two caliber, and it looked like a boy from Pekin school."

"I'm Mark Watson and this is my partner Tom Damon. They're physically fit and stand about six foot one inch. Officer Watson has red hair, brown eyes and a clean-shaven face. Officer Damon has light brown hair, blue eyes and a mustache. Their uniforms feature the City of Peoria insignias, and they carry thirty-eight caliber weapons at their side.

"Are you able to give us a description of the boy?" asks Officer Watson.

"The boy was about my son's height and wore a t-shirt with the Cardinals logo printed on the front," says Father.

"This boy looked like the one that charged the mound where Russel pitched before," says Mother.

"How are you, Russel; are you ready to talk?" asks Officer Damon.

"Ouch! My leg!" I say, holding my leg.

"We'll talk when you get better," says Officer Watson.

"We're all set," says a parametic as the ambulance takes me to the hospital.

"It's okay Russel, we're here with you," says mother.

"Tom, Charles, and Donna are coming because I sent a text to them about what happened."

"I can't wait to get out of here," I say, sitting in a hospital room.

The local news comes on TV: "Hello everyone, I'm Harry Walters from the local television station with our top story. A boy has been shot near his home by the University. The police have not disclosed any details yet, pending further investigation. If you have any information regarding this shooting, please call the local authorities. This is Harry Walters reporting."

I spend three days in the hospital, and went through a successful operation. Mom and Dad told me that I would make a full recovery. The weather is a little cloudy when I leave for home. My parents are in the living room watching the news when the phone rings and my father picks up the receiver.

"Hello, this is the Smith residence."

"This is Mr. Swanson; how is Russel?" he asks.

"Russel is doing fine, and how's everything, Mr. Swanson?" asks Father.

"It's okay, Charles, I'm in contact with the lawyer for the Little League. They are willing to negotiate letting Russel pitch; therefore, congratulations, Mr. and Mrs. Smith," speaks Mr. Swanson.

"What happens next?" asks mother. "I'll let you know when I meet with Mr. James with the details," says Mr. Swanson.

I'm playing with some CDs when my parents get off the phone with Mr. Swanson. "Do I get to play?" I ask.

"Hold on, son, we'll find out soon," says Father.

Suddenly, there is a knock at the door.

"Who is it?" asks my father.

"It's Officers Damon and Watson," says Watson. They come in and sit down.

"Would you gentlemen want some coffee?" asks Mrs. Smith.

"That will be fine," remarks Mr. Damon. Mother brings in coffee while the four adults gather around the dining room table.

"What brings you by?" asks father.

"Mr. Smith, the reason we're here is that we conducted our investigation and have found the gun that was used to shoot your son," says Officer Damon.

"Where is it?" asks mother.

"We have a warrant to search the home of Mr. Brian Sampson. Can we talk to Russel?" asks Watson.

"Russel, these officers want to talk to you," says father.

"What is it?" I ask with a curious voice.

"What happened between you and the kid from Pekin school?" asks Officer Watson.

"I was pitching, and I remember getting my first strikeout. I got scared because I'm told that boy charges the mound," I speak.

"How is it you're able to pitch?" asks Officer Damon.

"I'm sorry, Mr. Damon, Russel has light perception, and we adapted a pair of earbuds with a hearing aid so the catcher can use a wireless microphone to relay what type of pitches and where the ball should be thrown to keep the batters off balance," speaks my father.

"That's interesting Russel, and we wish you success," speaks Mr. Watson. The 2 policemen give their cards, exchange hand-shakes, and head back to the station.

Chapter 4

Mom and Dad get me ready for Little League and I experience one of my most embarrassing defeats.

"This is Harry Walters reporting. We are here because Russel Smith is pitching his fifteenth game in Little League. Butch Lang is catching for this young man and is recovering from a gunshot in the leg."

"Russel, need a fastball," whispers Butch into the microphone.

"There is a fastball, and the game is underway," reports Mr. Walters. "Here comes the 0 and 1 count: swing, and there's a drive, way back, and outta here for a home run, and the Iowa Little League takes a one-run lead."

"Oh man, what an idiot!" I speak while stamping my feet in frustration.

Coach Patterson comes out of the dugout and walks to my catcher. "It's my fault, Coach," speaks Butch.

"How is Russel, Butch?" asks Mr. Patterson.

"He's okay, I think," speaks Butch.

Coach Patterson walks to me. "Russel, it's Coach Patterson, are you all right?" he asks. "We're in the fifth inning one run down."

"My fastball is not right, and my curveball is not curving," I speak.

"Look son, there are days like this. I'll get somebody warmed up and get through somehow," speaks Coach Patterson. The weather for the game is breezy, with the temperature around eighty-three degrees.

"This is Harry Walters reporting. We're breaking from the game to tell you that a minor from Pekin School has been arrested in connection with the shooting of Russel Smith. A twenty-two caliber pistol was recovered from the home. A court date is set for July 2. His identity is being withheld, and has says that his brother shot Russel."

"Let's go back to the game with Smith facing Kurt Ramos, batting 275 with 40 runs batted in. Here's the first pitch: swing and a miss. Lang signals Smith to deal a curve ball: swing and there's a drive, way back, outfield looking toward the wall for another home run. Coach Patterson is walking back to the mound and it appears that he has Mike Nox warming in the bullpen."

"We're sorry Russel, we have to take you out," says Mr. Patterson to me and grabs the ball for Mike Nox. I walked back with him because I know I didn't have a good performance.

"It's okay Russ, we'll get you to the Majors one day," says father. The day gets a little darker as the afternoon progresses with the temperature dropping below eighty degrees.

⚾ ⚾ ⚾

I manage to straighten out and have a winning record in Little League and move on to the Little League World Series where I have one of my best moments. Mexico is the team we're playing against with the Series on the line.

"This is Harry Walters live from Chicago with a special report. It is reported that a trial date for the alleged shooter is scheduled for July second, but due to the postseason for the Little League, his trial has been moved to September 9th. We continue with Russel Smith warming up to make his first start against the Mexican Little League. Let's go to the field for an interview."

"This is Scott Wilcox here with Russel Smith and his parents before he takes the mound against Mexico. What is your mindset going against these guys?"

I reply, "I'm nervous but ready to face these guys and win the Series."

Mr. Wilcox says, "You folks must be proud of what your son has accomplished. What are your plans after the Series?"

"We plan on resting Russel and getting him ready for junior high school, and on to high school, where he'll graduate and go to the Minors," says father.

"Thank you and good luck," speaks Scott Wilcox.

Donna, Tom, Charles Jr. and my parents look on as I take the mound with my device and earbuds. "This is Dale Magnussen announcing as Russel Smith faces Edwardo Heminez. And here's the first pitch: curveball low and outside. Butch Lang is Russel's best friend and catcher."

"Curveball Russ," he whispers into the wireless microphone. He deals the next pitch: swing and a miss. Heminez stares out at the mound as Smith delivers: swing and a bouncer to the shortstop and throws to first for the out." The game continues in the bottom of the ninth inning with the Peoria and Mexican Little League scoreless and Butch Lang batting 250 with 35 runs batted in.

"Here's the first pitch from Miguel Lopez: swing and a miss," reports Harry Walters. "We've got a 0 and 1 count: swing, and there's a drive, way back, it's long enough and gone for the game-winning home run! Wow, what a scene!"

I move in the crowd as we win the Series and the family give me hugs of congratulations on a good game. The cameras click as reporters line up and chant my name for questions.

"Hello this is Dave Anderson and we're with Russel Smith. Can you tell us, young man, how this feels and what are your future plans because of your vision loss?"

I speak, "I want to play baseball like everybody else and be in the Majors one day."

"That is so cool. How does your son feel about the pressure facing opposition from people who say that visually impaired people can't do anything?" asks Mike Norris, another reporter.

Father replies, "He maintains a positive attitude and doesn't let anyone tell him he can't do whatever he puts his mind to. It's about adapting to the situation and supporting him to make the best of his abilities."

"Hello, son, this is Bruce Morris. You pitch a fine game with a three-hit shut-out; why are you so effective?" asks Mr. Morris.

I reply, "My fastball is in control, and my teammates tell me I have command of my curveball and mixing pitches to keep these guys off balance. But my teammates play well to win the game."

"This is Dave Anderson, live from Chicago, and good afternoon." Everyone scatters from the press conference and heads in different directions.

My parents and I go home to get ready for junior high school, where there is another hurdle.

Chapter 5

"When do I get to play?" I ask.

"The junior high school is dealing with visually impaired people for the first time," speaks mother.

I'm angry that Principal Doud won't let me play baseball because I'm blind.

"We have to deal with this, Russ, because people are still learning about visual impairment," explains Father somberly.

"I thought we were moving on from that," I tell him.

The phone rings, and my father picks up the receiver.

"Hello, this is Mr. Smith," says Father.

"Hi, this is Mr. Swanson we need to have Russel testify against Brian Sampson," he says on the line.

"We'll be ready, Mr. Swanson," Father speaks.

I'm nervous as I ride with Mom and Dad to the courthouse, described as an auditorium with seating around a platform useful for the judge and lawyers representing their clients.

"Hi Russel, this is Mr. Swanson how are you feeling?" asks Mr. Swanson greeting us at the door to the courthouse. "I've seen you pitch in the Little League World Series."

"I'm a little nervous, but the Series is great," I say excitedly.

"It's okay, young man. We need your story to convince the jury that this young man needs anger management for his problems," speaks Mr. Swanson.

There is a lot of chattering among the crowd before Judge Weldon Burk bangs his gavel. Mr. Burk is five foot ten, with gray hair, brown eyes, a clean-shaven face and 225 pounds. He wears a white dress shirt, brown dress pants and a black robe over his clothes.

"Order in the court!" the bailiff announces in a deep commanding voice. The crowd settles down as the proceedings begin, with the weather outside becoming cloudy and sixty-five degrees as Fall approaches.

"We begin with opening statements from the prosecution and defense. We expect both sides to be professional beginning with the prosecutor and defense attorney. Will Travis Barnes begin, please?" asks Judge Burk.

"I'm scared, Dad," I whisper.

"Look, son; it's all right; we're here for you. This is how court conducts business beginning with opening statements, trial and closing arguments," says father.

Mr. Barnes stands up to speak: "This young man you see before you is troubled and needs help before he goes further down a life of crime. I recommend that he spend time in juvenile prison for shooting Russel Smith. Mr. Smith is a young man who pitches baseball and wants to represent our community. There are other issues in the past for the young defendant because the parents are doing the best job for the young lad. I hope you're fair in examining the evidence showing that the defendant needs guidance." Mr. Barnes sits down in his chair and stretches out his long legs. He's six foot four, with short blond hair, blue eyes and 185 pounds. He has a dark brown dress shirt, brown dress pants and sports jacket.

William Finch stands up to speak, "Ladies and gentlemen of the jury, this young man before us is very apologetic for his actions against Russel Smith. He's innocent because his brother is the one who pulled the trigger and is missing. The fingerprints on the gun don't match my client and he's sorry for what happened. I hope you're fair in your assessment of the evidence so the defendant can continue his life and learn from this experience."

Mr. Finch sits down in his chair with his hands folded across his lap. Bill Finch is six foot with light brown hair, hazel eyes and weighs 195 pounds, wearing a white dress shirt, black dress pants and black dress shoes.

I sit patiently as Judge Burk speaks: "Mr. Barnes, do you have your first witness?"

Mr. Barnes stands to speak: "My first witness is Officer Thomas Damon from the Peoria Police Department." The crowd talks softly as Mr. Damon makes his way toward the stage area.

"Please raise your right hand. Do you swear to tell the truth?" asks the bailiff.

"I do," speaks Officer Damon.

"State your name and occupation for the record," says Judge Burk.

"I'm Thomas Damon and I have worked for the police department for sixteen years."

"Mr. Damon, describe the scene for us when you arrived on the scene of the shooting," asks Mr. Barnes.

"The parents were doing a fine job of calming our victim. Officer Watson and I gathered information that the shooting. The victim's mother reported that it may have stemmed from an incident where the victim pitched during the game between Pekin and Thomas Jefferson School. This alleged gunman was angry because he struck out."

"Objection, your honor, the prosecution has information that we don't know about," speaks Mr. Finch.

"Overruled, you don't need to argue. Mr. Barnes you may continue," speaks Judge Burk.

"Officer Damon, is it possible that the defendant's brother has something to do with the shooting?" asks Mr. Barnes.

"No, because the defendant's brother was away visiting a friend when the shooting took place," speaks Mr. Damon.

"Ladies and gentlemen of the jury, observe an exhibit that shows the gun and the defendant's brother's fingerprints match the prints on the handle," speaks Mr. Barnes.

"No more questions, your honor." speaks Mr. Barnes.

"Are you ready to cross-examine Mr. Finch?" says Judge Burk.

"Yes, thank you. Officer Damon, you say that the defendant's brother was away visiting a friend. Where does the friend live?" asks Mr. Finch.

"Mr. Finch, this is awkward. The defendant's brother lives across the street from the Smith residence, and we talked to everyone around the area. The gun was recovered from the home of the defendant," answers Mr. Damon.

"That means it's possible that you took the gun and planted the evidence to frame my client," speaks Mr. Finch.

"That's not true! It's insulting to downgrade my job!" speaks Mr. Damon with emotion.

"Objection, your honor, the defense is accusing the local police of evidence tampering," argues Mr. Barnes.

"Sidebar, gentlemen!" commands Judge Burk. The two lawyers glare at each other as they approach the Judge.

"Look, gentlemen, need I remind you that we have women and children in the crowd, and Mr. Finch, you're to be careful about planting improper seeds in the jury's mind because your livelihood depends on evidence."

"Your Honor, I apologize, but I think it could be a possibility," says Mr. Finch.

"Let's proceed," reminds Judge Burk.

The lawyers go back to their respective chairs while Officer Damon waits patiently.

"Russel, are you okay?" asks Mr. Swanson.

"I'm a little nervous." I reply.

"When you're done testifying, we'll get home and get you ready for junior high school baseball," reassures father. I feel relief to hear that and relax as the trial moves onward.

"Mr. Damon, I see that Mr. Smith is visually impaired. Is that correct?" asks Mr. Finch.

"Yes sir, he is," says Mr. Damon.

"That's all, your honor." speaks Mr. Finch.

"Thanks for your service, Officer Damon, you may step down," speaks Judge Burk. Officer Damon goes back to his seat while the crowd talks softly, and Judge Burk looks over his notes.

"Ladies and gentlemen, it's time for lunch and court resumes at one o'clock." says Judge Burk. Everyone empties the courtroom in all directions, and we head to find McDonald's, a fast-food restaurant, for a bite. I ordered an Angus burger with cheese, mustard, onion, lettuce and tomato, my dad ordered a cheeseburger with fries, and mom orders a salad and a medium coke.

"How are you, Russ?" asks my father.

"It's okay, Dad. I'm nervous about testifying." I say with a little tension. It's time to return to court and resume trial with everybody filling seats and Judge Burk banging his gavel.

"Order in the court! Are you ready for your next witness?" he asks.

Mr. Barnes speaks: "We call Russel Smith to the stand." The crowd talks softly as Mr. Swanson leads me to the platform.

"Raise your right hand please, do you swear to tell the truth under oath?" asks the bailiff.

"Yes, I do, your honor," I say.

"State your name and where you go to school, son," speaks Judge Burk.

"I'm Russel Smith and Thomas Jefferson School is where I pitch baseball," I reply.

"Russel, this is Mr. Barnes. Are you aware of who shot you, and do you think it's the same boy who strikes out against you?" asks Mr. Barnes.

"Yes, Mr. Barnes, but I'm a little nervous because he charges the mound, and the umpire stops him," I reply.

"Can you tell us what happened that day when you were pitching for the school, please?" asks Mr. Barnes.

"Objection, your honor, that question has no bearing on why my client is here today!" says Mr. Finch.

"Overruled answer the question, son," speaks Judge Burk.

"I'm scared because the batter strikes out, and he charges the mound, and my catcher tells me the umpire gets to him before he starts something. I'm told later that his coach leads him away, and the dude is still angry." I answer.

"Did he say anything to you?" asks Mr. Barnes. The defendant sits in his chair, hands folded across his lap, and a face that shows no emotion as he listens to the testimonies.

He yells, "That's not fair! You stupid jerk!" I answer. The crowd talks as the defendant suddenly jumps up and starts swinging his fists toward where Russel is testifying.

"Order! Order in the court!" commands Judge Burk as he bangs his gavel. "Sit down, Mr. Sampson, before you're held in contempt!"

He disobeys, resulting in the bailiffs removing the defendant by force from the courtroom and sending him back to his cell.

"I'm sorry ladies and gentlemen, for the delay, but that is uncalled for. Let's proceed," said Judge Burk.

"Can you tell us what was happening during and after the shooting?" asks Mr. Barnes.

I try to stay calm as I say, "I was getting out of the car, and then I remember that my dad told me to stay calm, but I was in pain and hit by the sound of a gun and then my leg hurt bad. My mom told me that they were there with me and yelled for someone to call 911. I remember the cops asking Dad to describe what he saw

"Do you know the name of the boy and where he goes to school?" asks Mr. Barnes.

"Objection your honor, that is not relevant. We know who he is, and let's move on," speaks Mr. Finch.

"Sustained, you don't need to answer the question," says Judge Burk.

"Statement withdrawn," says Mr. Barnes.

"That's it, your honor," Mr. Barnes says, and sits down.

"Do you have anything for the witness?" asks Judge Burk.

"Hi Russel, I'm Mr. Finch. I hear you like baseball. Are you sure of what happens when you say the batter strikes out against you?" asks Mr. Finch.

"Yes, I'm sure about what ,happens," I tell him.

"What is that?"

"The batter is out. If there haven't been three outs, then the next batter comes to the plate. If the batter is the third out in the inning, then the two sides switch places."

"Thank you," Mr. Finch says. He paused and walked in front of me, then continued, "When the shooting occurred, are you aware that you may be misinformed as to what happened because of your lack of sight?" asked Mr. Finch.

"Objection, your honor. The defense is using blindness as an issue," spoke Mr. Barnes.

"Sustained, that question will be stricken from the record," speaks Judge Burk.

"Look, son, we want to inform you so that Brian can learn from this and move on with his life," says Mr. Finch. "That's all, your honor."

"Thank you, son, and step down. You're a very courageous young man," speaks Judge Burk.

The wind is fifteen miles an hour coming from the south as my parents lead me out from the courtroom, and I breathe a sigh of relief. We head to the car. "You did a fine job my son," says mother.

"I'm glad it's over. I want to play baseball," I say. The rest of the day is spent preparing to register at the junior high school and go to the gym.

"This is Marlin Fox reporting from the Peoria courthouse. The testimonies of the witnesses including Russel Smith have ended. The defense in the trial of the accused start their testimonies. The case has been given to the jury and they have begun deliberating. When a verdict is returned we will keep you updated. Marlin Fox reporting."

"My name is on the news all the time. Why is that?" I ask.

"Russ, when you are working hard to achieve your goals, society puts entertainers in the spotlight because of their accomplishments. It's best that we pray and keep a positive attitude about you becoming a Major League pitcher one day," answers father.

The night comes quickly we go to sleep. There is a storm passing through, with winds gusting to thirty miles, lots of rain, and pea-sized hail. The thunder roars and lightning cracks for an hour, but there is minor damage as the storm moves out of the area.

Chapter 6

I've started junior high school for the first time as the case was winding down. I'm ready to resume baseball.

"This is Marlin Fox reporting. The accused shooter in the Russel Smith attack has been charged as an adult. Brian Sampson has been found guilty by a jury of his peers and is sentenced to prison for twenty-five years. This is Marlin Fox reporting from the County Jail."

"Wow, what a twist of events!" I tell Dad.

"It goes to show that violence doesn't solve problems," says Father.

There was another humbling moment because I discovered that the wrestling team has another visually impaired person at Peoria Central, and Mr. Stewart, my baseball coach, is willing to take a chance.

"I like your grades Russel, and Mr. Doud is willing to accept you as part of the team," speaks Mr. Stewart.

"Thank you, sir," I answer. Mr. Stewart has blond hair, blue eyes and stands six foot, 195 pounds. He wears a uniform with the school logo on the front, brown pants and athletic shoes.

The teammates cheer when I take part in warm-ups on the field with my speaker and earphones.

"That's pretty cool," Chad Hutson says. Chad is medium build, about five foot three, black hair, dark blue eyes and 157 pounds, wearing a uniform with the junior high school logo.

"Guys, we're here to win games and not worry about distractions," Coach Stewart said.

We prepare to go onto the field.

"We're here to watch Russel Smith pitch on the bump for the Peoria Central Lions as they start their baseball season. We wait as Russel does warm-up tosses," announces Marlin Fox.

"Hi Russel, it's Butch, are you ready?" he asks when he reaches the mound.

"What did you do to your arm, it's swollen?" Butch says with concern. Butch played with Russel in Little League.

"Oh no! No!" I exclaim with frustration. Coach Stewart and the trainer, Scott Hopkins led me off the mound, through the field and toward the locker room.

"Ladies and gentlemen, Russel Smith is leaving the field with an injury, and we're not sure what it is. We'll give you the details when we get more information. This is the local station reporting." says Marlin Fox.

"What happened, Russ? Are you all right?" asks Mother as she came into the locker room.

"It's my arm, I feel some pain and Butch tells me it's swelled," I say.

"You're on the fifteen day disabled list for now, and we'll have you checked," speaks Mr. Scott Hopkins. Mr. Scott Hopkins is listed at six foot, with brown hair, blue eyes, and wearing the uniform with the lion on the front with the word "Central" on the back. He wears brown dress pants and athletic shoes.

An appointment is made for me to see Dr. Shawn Hamilton, who specializes in sports injuries.

"I'm so disappointed; what do I do now?" I ask.

"It's okay, Russ, stay positive, and we'll get this straightened out and have you back in pitching form again," explains Father.

"This is a setback; we know things will happen. Your arm may be overused because of the season and the Little League World Series. This could happen to anyone. Stay positive, son."

I relax as the nurse enters the waiting room"Russel Smith, please," he says.

Mother leads me back to the exam room where the doctor meets his patients. The room itself is fifty-five feet by fifty feet with an adjustable bed, medical supplies for blood pressure, and other necessities. "I'm Mr. Young; what seems to be the trouble?" asks the nurse.

"It's my arm, I pitch baseball," I say. The blood pressure is taken to be sure it's okay, and I'm told to wait for .Dr. Shawn Hamilton.

Dr. Hamilton appears, wearing a light brown dress shirt, brown dress pants and brown dress shoes. He stands five feet eleven, muscular, 225 pounds, with a clean-shaven face, blond hair, and blue eyes. He smiles after he walks in to speak. "The nurse tells me you have a problem with your arm, is that right?" the doctor asks with a friendly tone.

"Yes, I was doing warm-ups with my catcher when I felt pain there," I say.

"Tell me more, Mr. Smith," he speaks with interest.

"I just started pitching for the Central Lions," I say.

Doctor Hamilton said, "Oh, that's right. , You play baseball. I have seen you on TV. Your arm is important then, and X-rays will show what's going on. How is the Little League World Series?" he asks.

"It's fun. I look forward to making the Big Leagues," I say.

The doctor reviews the x-rays and prescribes some ibuprofen and tells me to see him in a week.

The next week, I'm back to see Doctor Hamilton, and he has plenty of information. "Your parents can be with us as we talk," says Dr. Hamilton. "Russel, I have good news, and bad news. The good news is you'll make a full recovery, but the bad news is you need surgery to repair a ligament."

"How long will I be out?" I ask.

"That depends on your body, and your willingness for rehabilitation to recover. It's anywhere from three to six months, and the rehabilitation is important," says Doctor Hamilton.

"Will it be a long operation?" asks my father.

"No, roughly about two or three hours. The surgery is scheduled for next month, it'll be performed by Dr. Mitch Morris. You'll get your instructions closer to surgery, butbe sure not to eat or drink twelve hours before the operation," advises Doctor Hamilton."

I am disappointed by the results, but I have to face the fact that there is a long recovery ahead.

⚾ ⚾ ⚾

The next month arrives, and I'm brought in for surgery early in the morning, roughly about eight o'clock. My family is there, waiting for me to go.

"It's okay, Russel; I know you're scared, but we're here for you," advises Mother. "Keep praying and you'll be fine."

I relax as Tom, Charles, and Donna joke with me while they prepare me for surgery.

"Look at that cart," Tom laughs as he points toward the surgery cart. The cart is long and skinny, roughly six feet long and two feet wide, so the surgeon can move around easily.

"Good luck, brother," says Donna.

"Don't fall off," jokes Charles as the hospital staff takes me away down the hall to the room for surgery. I don't remember a lot, but I remember the nurse put a mask over my face with the anesthesia to put me to sleep.

An hour later, Dr. Morris went to the waiting room where my family sits waiting for news.

"Hello everyone, Mr. and Mrs. Smith. Russel is recovering. We successfully repaired the damaged ligament."

"Thank you, Doctor," my father says with relief.

"Let's go eat," says Mother. My family goes to the cafeteria for an hour and comes back to the waiting room while I recover. Doctor Morris comes out an hour and a half later with the news.

"Mr. and Mrs. Smith, Russel is doing fine. The operation is a success, and the ligament is repaired, he's waking up. Now the long road begins. It's up to him to get his strength back."

"Russel will be glad," says Mother. I wake up about an hour later and my family is there waiting to greet me. The bed has a device that looks like a remote control with a button to induce pain medication when I need it.

"Russ, it's Dad. how are you feeling?" asks my father.

"I'm groggy, but glad to be out of surgery." I say, mumbling.

"We'll. We'll be back; let's leave him alone," says the Mother.

Mom, Dad, and the rest of the family say their goodbyes and leave the hospital so I can rest. I'm in the hospital for three days, and then discharged to begin my rehabilitation.

Mr. Jeff Wilson gives me some instructions for a routine. Mr. Wilson is a physical therapist who's six feet tall, with red hair, blue eyes, and 205 pounds. "Hello Russel. In order to re- cover, you need to come to the hospital and work on the tread- mill, sit in a chair with arm pedals, and stretch out as much as you can to keep your arms loose." I'm also instructed to keep on a good diet and drink lots of fluids, but it is hard not being able to play with the rest of my teammates on the field.

Chapter 7

This routine takes me three and a half months, and now I'm ready to join my team at the local junior high school for the first time. "Look who's here!" remarks Butch excitedly.

Coach Stewart comes over. "Hi Russel; ready for a new season?" he asks.

"I'm feeling good," I say.

"Hello everyone, we're to see Russel pitch for the new season at the local junior high school," announces Harry Walters and continues, "We've got a crowd of about fifteen hundred people here to witness the action. It's a beautiful day for baseball, the temperature is seventy degrees and very little wind."

"The field is in tip-top shape, and the umpires are ready for the game," remarks the commentator, Ron Combs.

"Here we go, the crowd cheers and claps as Russel steps to the mound for the first pitch," says Harry Walters.

"Smith deals, curveball low and inside. Let me ask you, Ron, why is he wearing earbuds?" asks Harry Walters.

"Russel Smith's pitch is low and out of the strike zone," says Ron.

"The reason for the earbuds is not because of distraction, but for the catcher to let him know the pitches to throw to the batters."

Harry Walters speaks, "Here comes the one, zero pitch. Swing and a miss for strike one."

"He seems nervous, but throwing excellent pitches," speaks Ron Combs. "He looks ready for the pros right now."

"That's pretty cool how he…a swing and a ground ball to the shortstop and throws to first for the out," speaks Harry.

"That is a beautiful fastball that sinks for the ground out," says Ron.

I'm happy that I threw a magnificent game, giving up one run, striking out seven, and walking only one batter.

"Here we have the star of the game. Congratulations, Russel, this is Harry Walters; how are you feeling?" he asks.

I say, "My arm feels fine, I'm ready for the season and move on to college, the Minors, and the Big Show."

"Tell the audience how you pitch, because not a lot of them know that you have no sight." says Ron.

"The thing is that I wear earbuds for the catcher to let me know what pitches to throw and how high or low to pitch because the catcher wears a wireless microphone like Bluetooth technology."

"Tell us more about your mindset before the game," says Ron.

"I'm worried about my arm and whether I would perform well before the injury, and here I am after beating East Peoria Junior High School after my injury. It's a great feeling." I say.

"Thank you for your time, Mr. Smith, and we'll let you join your parents, who are waiting patiently."speaks Harry Walters.

"Thank you for having me," I say. The field scatters in all directions as everyone continues on to other things.

I manage to stay injury-free throughout the season, and have a winning record going into the championship game.

"Welcome, everyone, to the Junior High School championship between Peoria and Springfield," Harry Walters says. "The wind is coming from the south at five to eight miles with the grass cut short on the field, and standing room only and the crowd about ten to twelve thousand to see Russel Smith pitch."

"That's correct, Harry," continues Ron Combs. "This facility is plush green and ready for baseball."

This is a good moment for me, but it didn't start out that way.

"Smith is ready for the first inning as he deals: swing and a single up the middle from Blake Griffith of Springfield," Harry Walters announces.

"He has lost command of his fastball," Ron continues. "Maybe it's nerves, hopefully Smith will straighten out."

"Brian Cush steps to the plate: swing and a long drive, way back, way back, and gone," Harry speaks, dejected.

Ron speaks, "It's up to the rest of the team to help Russel." I'm disappointed when coach Stewart comes to the mound. "Russ, it's me Coach Stewart, how are you feeling?"

"I don't realize how tired I am," I say.

"Hang in there, we know the rest of the team should be able to step up and help you now," Coach Stewart advises. "I'm leaving you in the game to straighten out for now and good luck." Coach Stewart walks back to the dugout as I relax.

Butch speaks into the microphone, "Need a curveball low."

"Smith deals: swing and a miss by Dave Thomson," Harry announces.

"That is a beautiful curveball low and outside, and this is Russel Smith we're used to," says Ron Combs.

The crowd watched as I pitched the rest of the game with a good performance, but I didn't figure in the win. We're still tied when Butch Lang comes to the plate with the score two to two.

"Here's Butch Lang at the plate," speaks Harry.

"The crowd is at the edge of their seats as Lang waits for the first pitch from Troy Hawkins: swing and a single up the middle for the next batter, Weldon Schmidt. Schmidt is Peoria's home run leader with twenty home runs, and stands six foot and 225 pounds. He swings and a drive, long and deep, and outa here for a two-run blast! Wow, what a scene!"

I jump for joy as the cameras click, and all the media watches as the crowd cheers loudly.

"What a win for Peoria, as the score becomes four to two!" Walters speaks, "We're proud to be joined now by the star of the game, Weldon Schmidt."

"Tell us, Weldon, how do you get hot at that moment?" Harry asks.

"I want to thank Russel for encouraging me because we're down at one time two to zero. He tells me, "Weldon, you can do this." Luckily, I see the fastball coming my way; when I strike it, I know that ball is gone."

"You think Russel has a chance to be in the Majors; your thoughts?" asks Ron.

"I certainly do," Weldon continues, "He is very positive and a special athlete."

"Thanks for the time, and hope to see you guys again." Harry speaks.

"It's been a pleasure." Weldon Schmidt agrees.

I remember visiting Wrigley Field during the summer, as everyone around me describes the ivy on the back walls, the field is plush green with short grass, and the dugouts are state of the art, with a lounge and big lockers for the players to store their gear. I'm starting high school, and remember my best moments and worst moments.

The coach at the high school tells me visually impaired people can play sports. Coach Rivers is around five foot eleven, 195 pounds with blond hair, blue eyes and a uniform with the Warriors signature on the front. "I'm Coach Rivers; welcome to the team." Coach Rivers says to me.

"Remember there is no swearing, and you must keep your grades average and above."

"This is Harry Walters at the local high school where Russel Smith is to start his first game. The crowd is jammed, about five to six thousand people."

"It certainly is Harry. The field is well kept with the light wind coming from the south at seven to ten miles an hour," says Ron Combs. The crowd mills around by their seats trying to get a glimpse of my every move as I prepare for the game.

"Get ready folks, time for the stars to shine at the local high school." announces Harry Walters. "Tom Stanton comes to the plate for Peoria. He swings a long drive, back, back, and gone for a lead-off home run as Peoria takes its first lead in the game. The score is one to nothing in favor of Peoria against Morton High School."

"This is a good moment. But wait, the manager of Morton comes out to argue with the umpire Gerald Henson," speaks Ron combs.

"What an embarrassing moment, folks," adds Walters.

Mike Sloan, the manager of Morton High School comes out to read the umpire the riot act. "You stupid jerk, how dare you give the other team the advantage!"

The umpire speaks with authority, "Any more outbursts and you're out of the game!" The manager stalks back to the dugout, knowing he'd be thrown out. I stay in the game to continue pitching to the next batter.

"The wind up and the pitch, strike 1 with the curve," speaks Harry.

"What do you think, Ron?" asks Harry.

"Keep throwing curveballs down and away, like the last one," replies Ron Combs. The announcers keep talking as I continue to pitch well, with 8 strikeouts, 1 walk, and gave up 1 run, while Peoria wins 3 to 1.

"What a special moment as we wait to talk to Russel," says Harry.

"Here he is, we want to congratulate you on a fine performance, Russel," speaks Harry. "How are you feeling?"

"I'm a little tired, but I'll get through this," replies Russel.

"This is Ron Combs, Russel. We know you're visually impaired; you show courage and that is special to us," adds Ron.

"I appreciate that; it makes me feel good," I explain.

"How are you so effective," asks Ron.

"My teammates encourage me to stay positive and keep throwing pitches to keep the batters off balance," I reply.

"We'll let you go, and have a good rest of the year," says Harry. "That's all ladies and gentlemen, good night from the ballpark," announces Harry as the crowd disperses in all directions.

Chapter 8

Four years have passed, in what seems like a hurry, and finally, the draft.

"What a scene!" announces Mr. Gilbert, the master of ceremonies, at the facility near Wrigley Field. "We're here to announce a special moment in baseball history, the first legally or totally blind person will be drafted, will Russel Smith Stand up," speaks Mr. Gilbert. There is a large crowd in the building, with cameras clicking. Mr. Roger Gilbert is of average build, six foot tall, with blond hair, blue eyes, and 160 pounds, wearing a pinstriped suit.

"The envelope shows Russel Smith being drafted number 24 to play for the Chicago Cubs. Congratulations, Russel!" announces Mr. Gilbert.

Father guides me to the podium. "I want to congratulate everybody for the support that is given to me throughout my life," I say. "Thanks to my family, coaches, and teammates who helped along the way."

⚾ ⚾ ⚾

Food and drinks were served as the celebration continued throughout the night. My performance is good throughout two years in the Minors. The championship game is finally here, as I'm at Mynan field for a Minor League game with the Peoria, Cubs. This field is plush with short green grass. Inside, the locker room is well appointed. The wind is blowing around seven miles an hour out toward center field. It's packed with several thousand people for a glimpse of the action.

"Welcome to the championship for Peoria, against the Chicago White Sox affiliate," announces Harry Walters. "Alongside is Ron Combs, with his keys to the game."

"Hello everyone, for Peoria, they need to keep inducing ground balls from Russel Smith, forcing the Sox to be off balance, and on offense, Peoria should have key hits," speaks Ron.

"For the White Sox, their offense might be able to get to Smith, but he has been dominant throughout the year."

"There's a strike from Frank Martinez as the game is underway," announces Harry.

"The first batter looks ready," says Ron Coombs. "The batter for Peoria is Robert Martin, a five-foot eight right hander."

"Here comes the 1 strike pitch, a swing, and there's a long drive, way back, back, and long—outta here for a home run!' announces Mr. Walters.

"A beautiful swing by Martin as he lifts a fastball out in the middle of the plate," speaks Ron. Peoria holds a 1-nothing lead, as Butch Lambert comes to the plate. He's 5 foot 9 with long blond hair flowing from his baseball cap. His eyes are brown and he weighs in at 185 pounds.

"Here comes the pitch, Lambert swings and a single down the left field line," Harry continues, "that brings up Larry Hill, who used to play with Russel during grade school."

"He is a good fastball hitter and makes solid contact," adds Ron Coombs.

"Martinez seems like he only has a good fastball but no command," Harry announces, "Hill swings on the first pitch and drives this ball, back, back, and it's gotta chance.Long gone for a home run as Peoria takes a 3 to nothing lead, holy cow!"

The next 3 batters go down with a strikeout, ground ball, and another strikeout to get out of the inning. "We move to the bottom of the first, Russel Smith on the bump. What do you look for, Ron?" Harry asks.

"Russel features a fastball, curve, and changeup. Almost all of the batters rely on the fastball," says Ron.

"The first from Smith is a curve low and inside. Smith pitches with earbuds inside his cap, so the catcher can speak to him," announces Harry.

"A Beauty pitch right there as a strike," adds Ron. "LeRoy Jackson, a medium build man with brown hair and brown eyes, is at the plate for the White Sox as Russel pitches, swing and a miss," continues Harry.

"We like to thank all sponsors for this broadcast, and what a beautiful game," compliments Ron Coombs.

"Smith deals, a swing and a line drive whistles past him to the shortstop, who scoops it up, and throws to first for the out. What a play," Harry announces.

"Here comes a dangerous hitter, Jordan Springer." Ron Combs adds, "This man is a very good hitter for the White Sox, batting 299 with 77 runs batted in."

Harry Walters begins, "Russel is ready, ball low and inside."

"That pitch needed to be up a little more, but he has good command," compliments Ron.

Harry continues, Smith is into his windup, and delivers a swing and ground ball to the second baseman, picks the ball and throws to first for the out."

Smith's family is looking on as the game continues, "What a scene, Dad," says Tom. Just then, the phone rings.

"Hello, this is Mr. Smith. Can I help you?"

"This is Tim Swanson with the general manager of the Cubs."

"Hello, I'm Jeff Hoyer, general manager," speaks Mr. Hoyer on the line. "Your son is scheduled to make his Major League debut 2 days from now when the team comes back home from Milwaulkee. Congratulations to Russel."

When the game came to and end, I had thrown 105 pitches, striking out 7 and walked 2, with the score 3 to 2.

"What a moment, here is Russel to join us," says Harry. "How are you feeling Russell, how's your arm?" Harry asks.

"My arm feels good, and I just got the news I'll be heading to the Cubs!" speaks Russel with excitement.

"Simply awesome. Keep doing what you're doing, and you will be fine," adds Ron Combs. The celebration continues throughout the night after the game, and everyone departs later on.

Chapter 9

It's on to Chicago, where everyone gathered at Wrigley, roughly thirty-eight thousand people, for the arrival of the new star, Russel Smith.

Russel and the family are traveling north from Peoria to Chicago when a truck comes towards them at a high rate of speed, colliding with the vehicle near Rockford, Illinois, leaving the van a total loss. Everyone is still waiting for the game to begin, however there is a delay.

"Ladies and gentlemen, the game is called, because a wreck occurred near Rockford, Illinois, with the occupants still being identified," addresses the P.A. announcer.

Several minutes later, the general manager of the Cubs came over the loudspeaker. "Ladies and gentlemen, I just got off the phone with the Rockford police department, I'm sorry to report that Russel Smith and family has passed away from injuries from the wreck, where a truck collided with their car on the way to Chicago."

A hush fell over the crowd, understandably so. Over the next few days, wreaths and flowers are placed at the gravesite where Russel Smith and his family are laid to rest.

In the weeks that followed, the investigation of the wreck is ruled accidental, and Russel Smith's memory will go, as condolences come into the Chicago Cubs front office from all over the sports world.

Acknowledgments

There are many people I'd like to thank, but if I start naming names, other names could be left out. Thank you all.

About The Author

Anthony Engle was born to Shirley Engle, and his father is unknown, and has a brother and sister. He grew up in Peoria, Illinois, and currently works for Outlook Nebraska Incorporated and is a former employee of the year. My previous job was at the Business Enterprise Program for the Blind.

His influences are reading books, listening to old-time radio programs, and watching sports. He's married, has four stepchildren, several grandchildren, and great-grandchildren.